CANCER AND MODERN SCIENCE™

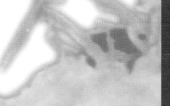

LYMPHOMA

Current and Emerging Trends in Detection and Treatment

JERI FREEDMAN

The Rosen Publishing Group, Inc., New York

616.991
FRE

Published in 2006 by The Rosen Publishing Group, Inc.
29 East 21st Street, New York, NY 10010

Library of Congress Cataloging-in-Publication Data

Freedman, Jeri.
Lymphoma: current and emerging trends in detection and treatment/
Jeri Freedman.
    p. cm.—(Cancer and modern science)
Includes bibliographical references and index.
ISBN 1-4042-0389-3 (library binding)
1. Lymphomas—Juvenile literature.
I. Title. II. Series.
RC280.L9F74 2006
616.99'446—dc22

2004030165

Manufactured in Malaysia

On the cover: A colored scanning electron micrograph of dividing Hodgkin's cells.

CONTENTS

INTRODUCTION

The story of lymphoma is, in many ways, the story of cancer itself. Although lymphoma was not the first cancer discovered, it was the first cancer to be treated successfully. The struggle to find a cure for this disease has resulted in the development of many of the standard treatments used for cancers of all types today.

The foundation was laid for modern trends in understanding and treating lymphoma when controlled clinical studies began to be conducted. These studies began to show clearly which treatments were effective. Then, proper analysis of patient populations and evaluation of the type and degree of the patients' disease established how to tailor treatments for specific patient groups. In addition, such studies highlighted the importance of sharing information among members of the medical community. Indeed, the input from many sources is necessary to find a cure for complex diseases such as lymphoma.

Advancements in technology, ranging from the discovery of X-rays to the use of mustard gas in the first and second world wars, have also

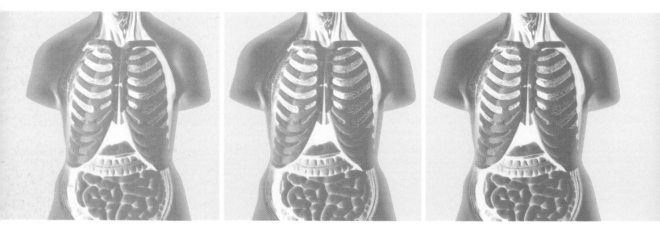

Students at Beverly Hills High School in Beverly Hills, California, run laps on May 6, 2003, while workers maintain the oil wells that are located under their campus. A complaint was filed against the oil company, the school district, and the City of Los Angeles by Erin Brockovich and her colleague Ed Masry. It stated that fumes leaking from these wells have caused 280 cases of both Hodgkin's and non-Hodgkin's lymphoma, as well as thyroid cancer since the 1970s. Brockovich's fight against environmental pollution was the inspiration for the film starring Julia Roberts in 2000.

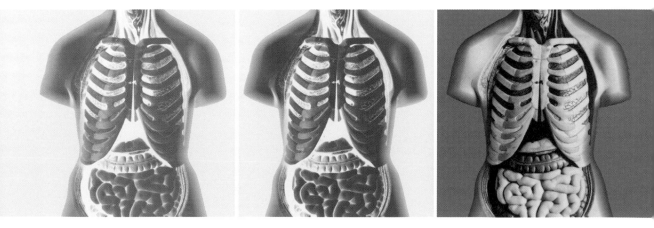

helped our understanding of lymphoma and have led to better treatments. Recent advances in genetic engineering have also been eagerly incorporated into our current efforts to understand and treat the disease.

Lymphoma is not a single disease. Rather, it is a group of various cancers that affect the lymphatic system, which is responsible for protecting the body from disease. Some types of lymphoma have been highly curable as a result of scientific advances in treatment; other types remain a puzzle to science. In the following chapters, we will explore this complex disease and its relation to modern science and technology.

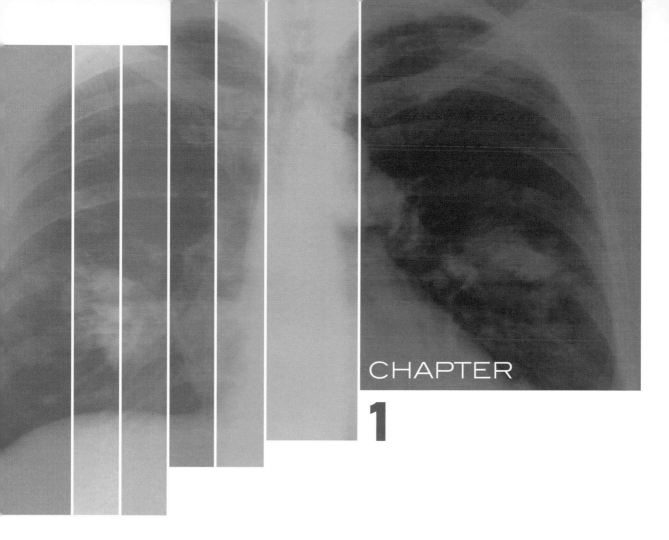

WHAT IS LYMPHOMA?

In the body, cells are constantly created. These cells then mature and die. Occasionally, however, instead of going through their normal life cycle, cells may keep dividing repeatedly, making new cells just like themselves. These are called clonal cells. It also happens occasionally that old cells don't die off as new cells are created. This results in an abnormally large clump of cells, which we call a tumor.

There are two types of tumors: benign and malignant. A benign tumor is a cluster of cells that builds up in the body but does not invade nearby tissue or spread to other parts of the body. Such

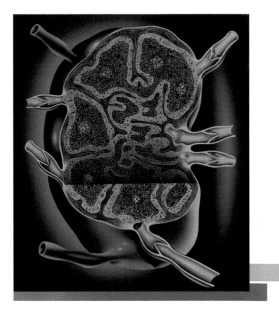

Here is an illustration of a human lymph node, which can be found at intervals along the lymph vessels of the human body. Usually, the kidney-shaped structure is about 1 inch (2.5 centimeters) in length, but this can vary throughout the body. The lymph node is surrounded by a thick, fibrous capsule. Entering and exiting the lymph node are lymph vessels, as well as arteries and veins.

tumors may cause discomfort and may need to be surgically removed. However, since they do not spread to other parts of the body, they generally are not considered harmful to the body. In contrast, cells that make up a malignant tumor not only grow out of control but also spread from the original tumor to other parts of the body. In these areas, they may continue to grow, creating new tumors. Eventually, if they are not stopped, malignant tumors can invade and affect major organs in the body, leading to death.

Lymphomas are one kind of malignant tumor. Lymphomas often start in the lymphatic system in locations such as the lymph nodes. They may then spread to other locations such as the lungs, liver, or bone marrow. There are two main categories of lymphoma: Hodgkin's disease, named after the doctor who first described it, and non-Hodgkin's lymphoma, which includes many different types of lymphoma that have characteristics that differ from Hodgkin's disease. Today Hodgkin's disease has well-established treatments and a very high cure rate. Because

HODGKIN'S DISEASE STATISTICS

— According to the American Cancer Society, in 2004, approximately 7,880 cases of Hodgkin's disease were diagnosed in the United States.

— Hodgkin's disease occurs most commonly in people in their twenties and thirties and in those older than fifty-five.

— Ten to 15 percent of cases involve people younger than the age of seventeen.

— In the past thirty years, death rates from Hodgkin's disease have fallen 60 percent because of improved treatments.

— As of 2004, 94 percent of children diagnosed with Hodgkin's disease can expect to survive for five years or more.

different types of non-Hodgkin's lymphoma exist, the treatments and cure rates vary, and a great deal of research is being directed at finding new and better treatments.

IN SEARCH OF THE RAMPAGING CELL

Although it was not the first cancer to be discovered, lymphoma was the first cancer that physicians tried to treat, and the first in which treatment was successful. Hodgkin's disease was first described by Italian anatomist and professor Marcello Malpighi (1628–1694) in 1666. He was the first to describe what we now know to be lymphoma in his book *De viscerum structura: exercitatio anatomica* (Concerning the Structure of the Viscera: Anatomical Exercises, London, 1669).

The man most closely associated with the discovery and description of lymphoma, however, is Dr. Thomas Hodgkin (1798–1866), a British

Thomas Hodgkin served as a professor of morbid anatomy at Guy's Hospital in London. Although he first described the disease in 1832, it wasn't until another prominent British physician, Samuel Wilks, became familiar with Hodgkin's published papers thirty-three years later in 1865 that the disease became known as Hodgkin's disease.

physician at Guy's Hospital in London. Ultimately, his studies of chest and abdominal tumors and how cancer spread resulted in a two-volume work on this subject. In 1832, he wrote a paper titled, "On the Morbid Appearances of the Absorbent Glands and Spleen," published in the journal of the Royal Medical and Chirurgical (surgical) Society of London. In this paper he described the type of lymphoma that now bears his name.

What is remarkable about Hodgkin's work is that he was able to distinguish this relatively rare disease from other more common lymphatic diseases, such as tuberculosis and leukemia, without performing microscopic studies. Hodgkin's original preparations of a tumor called *lymphogranulomatosis maligna* still exist at Guy's Hospital. When they were reexamined microscopically sixty years after his death, he was found to have been correct in his diagnosis of three of the cases he examined. The other four were non-Hodgkin's lymphomas, tuberculosis, or other lymphatic diseases.

Red blood cells, or erythrocytes, are pictured here. The bone marrow produces red blood cells, which then carry oxygen to the cells of the body and carry carbon dioxide away. When the red blood cell count is low, a patient is considered anemic, which can be a symptom of lymphoma. Although the red blood cell count is considered in diagnosing lymphoma, it cannot stand alone in the diagnosis.

ON THE TRAIL OF HODGKIN'S DISEASE

In 1856, Samuel Wilks, also a British physician, described ten cases of lymphoma, including three originally described by Hodgkin. In 1865, Wilks published more detailed observations in a paper titled "Cases of Enlargement of the Lymphatic Glands and Spleen." In recognition of Hodgkin as the first to describe the ailment, Wilks called this form of lymphoma "Hodgkin's disease." It is still known by this name today. Hodgkin had given very little description of the physical history of the patients from whom the samples he described were obtained. Wilks described the symptoms that those patients with the disease experienced in more detail, mentioning anemia, an abnormally low level of red blood cells, and intermittent fever. Pieter Pel, a Dutch physician, and Wilhelm Ebstein expanded on the nature of the fever that accompanies Hodgkin's disease. They described the cyclical nature of this fever in 1885 and 1886, respectively: The patient experiences a high fever for several days. The fever then goes away, only to return a few days later, and this cycle repeats over and over. Today this type of fever is known as a Pel-Ebstein fever.

Throughout the 1860s, researchers in Europe observed and described "giant" cells. These cells are larger than normal cells and have two or three nuclei rather than the single nucleus that normal cells have. These cells will be discussed in more detail in chapter 3.

In 1878, William Smith Greenfield wrote a paper called "Specimens Illustrative of the Pathology of Lymphadenoma and Leukocythemia," which was published in the *Transactions of the Pathological Society of London*. In this paper, he made the first drawing of Hodgkin's disease cells as observed with a low-power microscope. The nature of the diseased cells typical of Hodgkin's disease was described in detail independently by Austrian pathologist Carl Sternberg (1872–1935) in 1898 and American researcher Dorothy Reed (one of the first women to attend Johns Hopkins School of Medicine in Baltimore, Maryland) in 1902. The giant cells with multiple nuclei that they described have been referred to as Reed-Sternberg cells ever since.

CLARIFYING THE PICTURE

The first major classification system for differentiating between the various forms of the disease was created in 1947 by H. Jackson and F. Parker Jr. They wrote a series of medical papers and a book titled *Hodgkin's Disease and Allied Disorders*. Parker and Jackson called the main type of lymphoma Hodgkin's granuloma. A granuloma is a type of tumor made up of immune cells, blood vessels, and fibroblasts. Fibroblasts are undeveloped cells that eventually become mature cells with specific

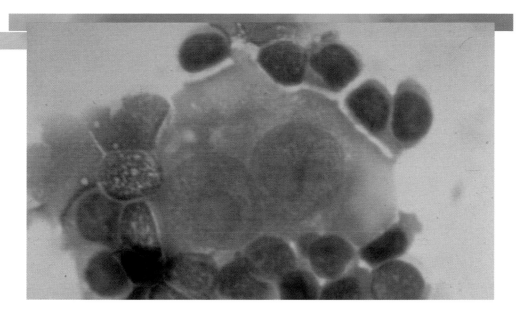

This is a photomicrograph of a Reed-Sternberg cell from a patient with Hodgkin's disease. The enlarged cell with its two nuclei is surrounded by lymphocytes. As the number of these B-cell derived malignant cells increase, the disease also advances. The presence of this cell is distinctively characteristic of Hodgkin's disease.

functions. A granuloma contains fibroblasts that would normally become connective tissues in the body, such as muscles and tendons.

Jackson and Parker assigned the name Hodgkin's sarcoma to a much more malignant form seen in a small number of cases. A sarcoma is a type of malignant tumor that grows in connective tissue such as muscle. Jackson and Parker used the term "Hodgkin's paragranuloma" ("near" granuloma) to describe a rare slow-growing form of Hodgkin's disease with few Reed-Sternberg cells. Twenty years later, in 1966, R. J. Lukes and J. J. Butler described another form, which was dubbed nodular sclerosis. In this type of Hodgkin's disease, bands of fibrous tissue divide the tissue into nodules, or clusters of cells.

When the disease was first studied in the late nineteenth and early twentieth century, researchers believed that it was somehow the result of infection. Various agents were suggested as the cause, including the bacteria associated with tuberculosis, diphtheria, encephalitis, and other diseases.

However, in the 1960s, studies of Hodgkin's disease cells proved that it is a type of cancer. From the 1970s to the present, a variety of scientific meetings have been held in the United States and Europe. There, researchers have shared new ideas about the nature, course, and treatment of lymphoma, as well as attempted to arrive at the best system for classifying the various forms of the disease.

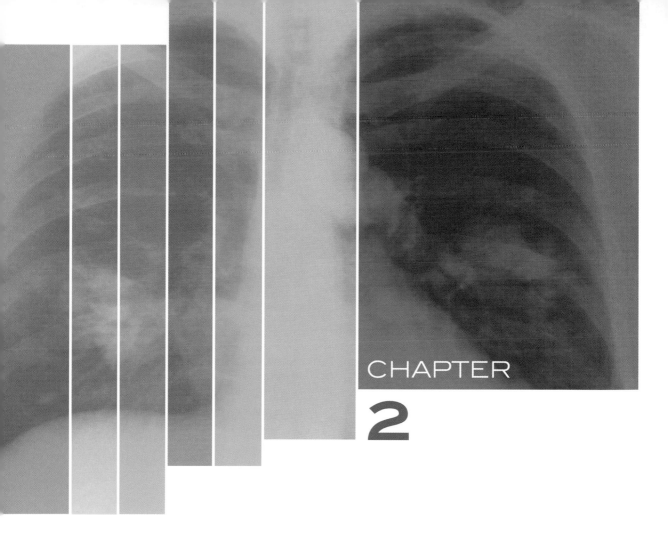

THE SCIENCE OF LYMPHOMA

To understand lymphoma, it is necessary to know a bit about the lymphatic system. This system of the body plays a major role in protecting us from infection. Lymphoma is a type of cancer that affects the lymphatic system.

ABOUT THE LYMPHATIC SYSTEM

The lymphatic system is a network of organs and vessels that produces and circulates a fluid called lymph. This fluid carries cells called lymphocytes that help defend the body against foreign agents. The

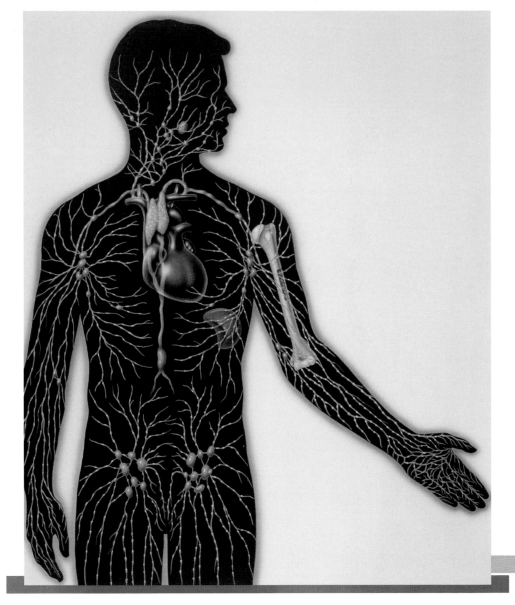

The lymphatic system, diagrammed here, is a subsystem of the circulatory system. Like blood vessels, lymph vessels branch throughout the body and, along with lymph capillaries, are found in the tissues of the body. Besides the immunity function, the lymph system absorbs excess fluid in the body as well as fat (lipids) in the villi of the small intestine.

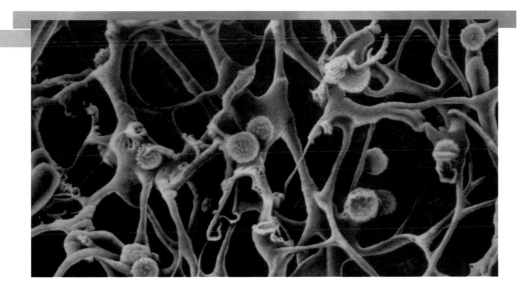

This is an illustration of a sectioned lymph node, based on an electron micrograph image. A lymph node is divided into compartments. In this image, the region of the medullary sinus, with its honeycomb of macrophages and reticular fibers, is shown. The function of this compartment is to slow the flow of lymphatic fluid through the node and facilitate the actions of the lymphocytes and their immune response processes.

lymphatic system is made up of bone marrow, the spleen, the thymus gland, lymph nodes, and tonsils. In the bone marrow at the center of our large bones, immune system cells are formed. The thymus gland is found in the upper chest area. The thymus consists of a framework of fibrous tissue filled with maturing lymphocytes. The thymus shrinks as the lymphocytes that compose it spread throughout the lymphatic system. The thymus also puts out thymosin, a hormone, which regulates the maturing of lymphatic tissue. This organ grows from birth through puberty. After puberty the thymus atrophies, or shrinks.

The lymphocytes move through our bodies in a series of tiny blood vessel–like tubes called capillaries. These tubes are filled with interstitial

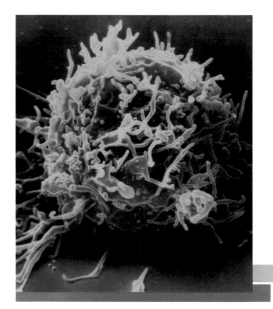

This is a scanning electron micrograph of a normal T cell. Long microvilli are found along the normal T cell's surface. T cells come from the bone marrow but differentiate, or specialize, in the thymus. There, they gain the ability to distinguish between what is another T cell, what is not, and what is to be attacked. This ability to recognize and memorize antigens is a key feature of the T cell.

fluid, a clear fluid that fills the spaces between our cells. This fluid seeps into the capillaries, providing a means of transporting the lymphocytes through the lymphatic system to the lymph nodes. Lymph nodes are honeycomb-like organs that contain clusters of immune system cells that attack foreign particles brought to the lymph nodes by the lymph.

The spleen is an organ located between the stomach and the diaphragm in the upper-left part of the abdomen. The spleen performs the same basic function as the lymph nodes, except that it filters foreign cells and particles out of blood circulating in the blood vessels rather than the lymph. In addition, it removes deformed and dead red blood cells from the body.

The tonsils are small organs filled with lymphocytes that are responsible for fighting microorganisms in the food we eat and the air we breathe as well as infections in the throat and nearby areas. In addition to the lymphocytes that travel in the lymph, some also travel back and forth between the lymph and blood. This circulation of lymphocytes helps make sure that when there is a foreign particle in the body, a lymphocyte programmed to attack it is likely to encounter it.

IMMUNE SYSTEM CELLS

There are two major types of lymphocytes: B cells and T cells, which use different types of mechanisms to recognize and attach to foreign agents. These foreign agents, such as bacteria, viruses, and other foreign particles, are referred to as the "target" of the B cells and T cells. The B cells and T cells start out as immature cells called stem cells that are produced in the bone marrow. As they mature, the B cells and T cells undergo changes that allow them to recognize and respond to specific targets. In B cells, genes that are responsible for the development of proteins called immunoglobulins are rearranged so that the B cell will recognize and respond to a particular type of target cell. In T cells, changes take place in the receptors (components on a cell that allow it to attach, or bind with, another cell or chemical molecule) on the outside of the cell that make it possible for them to attach themselves to specific targets. In the process of undergoing these changes something can go wrong with the T cells or B cells, causing them to grow out of control. We call this type of out-of-control cell growth cancer, and when this type of cancer occurs in the lymphatic system, it is known as lymphoma. Because of the specific changes that take place in different lymphocytes, it is possible for doctors and scientists to examine the cells in a lymphoma and see what particular population of cells caused it. This is helping scientists to understand what causes lymphoma and what might be done to cure it.

LYMPHOMA AND CELL REPRODUCTION

Most lymphomas come from B cells in various stages of development. Therefore, it's important to understand something about the structure of B cells, the role that genes play, and how they develop and reproduce.

There are two kinds of lymphatic tissue: central lymphatic tissue, found in the bone marrow and thymus, and peripheral lymphatic tissue, found in the spleen, lymph nodes, and mucous membranes in areas such as the throat, stomach, and intestines. Lymphocytes are created and mature in the central lymphatic tissue. The mature cells then travel to the peripheral lymphatic tissues and circulate through the body. As the mature cells come into contact with foreign agents, they undergo chemical changes in response, and this allows them to recognize and respond to these foreign targets when they encounter them again. The foreign agents that provoke a response in immune system cells are referred to as antigens.

OUT-OF-CONTROL GROWTH

The tumors produced in lymphoma are the result of uncontrolled cell growth caused by a change in or injury to a gene. The genes in our cells

STUDYING THE LYMPHATIC SYSTEM

During the seventeenth century, improvements in dissection tools and techniques made it possible for anatomists to gain new knowledge of the form and function of the human lymphatic system.

In 1692, Dutch anatomist Anton Nuck developed a technique for outlining the lymphatic system by injecting mercury into the lymphatic vessels of cadavers. In this technique a lymphatic vessel was punctured. Next a blowpipe was inserted and used to inflate the vessel. Then a brass or glass tube was inserted and used to fill the vessel with mercury. Modifications of this technique were used throughout the eighteenth, nineteenth, and early twentieth centuries to observe the layout of the lymphatic vessels.

carry all our hereditary information. Each gene basically carries the blue-print for a specific protein, one of the chemical compounds that make up our bodies.

There are two types of genes in the cells that cause tumors. The first type of gene is called a proto-oncogene. A proto-oncogene is a normal gene that can become a cancer-causing gene if it is damaged. Many such genes are normally responsible for producing compounds that control cell growth. Yet when this gene is changed or injured, it can become an oncogene, or cancer-causing, gene. It may cause increased production of a compound that causes cell growth, or decreased production of a com-pound that keeps too much growth from occurring.

The second type of gene is called a tumor suppressor gene. This type of gene stops, or suppresses, the action of another gene. If the suppres-sor gene becomes damaged and fails to do its job, the normally suppressed gene would no longer be suppressed, and this could lead to uncontrolled cell growth. The structure of lymphoma cells tends to remain the same after the cells undergo the genetic mutation, or change, that turns on the proto-oncogene or turns off the tumor sup-pressor gene. For example, a B cell can still be identified as that type of cell. For this reason, it is possible to examine the cells in a lymphoma to see from which type of cell the tumor originated. This allows doctors and researchers to understand exactly where the change that resulted in the tumor took place, which in turn helps in both understanding the cause of the disease and treating it.

CHAPTER 3

THE NATURE OF LYMPHOMA

Hodgkin's disease affects around 3 out of every 100,000 people in the United States. The key indicator of Hodgkin's disease is the appearance of the tumor of a particular type of malignant B cell called Reed-Sternberg (R-S) cells in lymphatic tissue or the lymph nodes. R-S cells are very large compared to normal cells. The main part of these cells is pale, and they have two or more nuclei (the part of cells that holds genetic material) as opposed to the single nucleus that normal cells have. The presence of these giant cells with their multiple nuclei is an important sign that a patient has

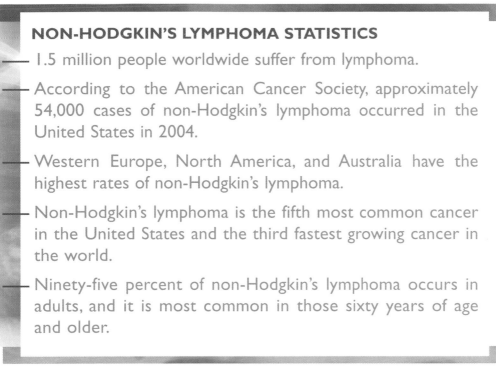

NON-HODGKIN'S LYMPHOMA STATISTICS

— 1.5 million people worldwide suffer from lymphoma.

— According to the American Cancer Society, approximately 54,000 cases of non-Hodgkin's lymphoma occurred in the United States in 2004.

— Western Europe, North America, and Australia have the highest rates of non-Hodgkin's lymphoma.

— Non-Hodgkin's lymphoma is the fifth most common cancer in the United States and the third fastest growing cancer in the world.

— Ninety-five percent of non-Hodgkin's lymphoma occurs in adults, and it is most common in those sixty years of age and older.

Hodgkin's disease rather than some other type of lymphatic disease such as tuberculosis.

SYMPTOMS OF HODGKIN'S DISEASE

One of the symptoms of Hodgkin's disease is swollen lymph nodes, sometimes referred to as swollen glands, that do not cause pain for the patient. These lymph nodes are located in the neck, under the arms, and in the groin. The disease may also cause swelling of the thymus in the chest. Because this gland is larger in children than in adults, the swelling caused by lymphoma may have effects in children not seen in adults. One of the signs of Hodgkin's disease in children is a cough that occurs for no apparent reason or shortness of breath. Some people suffering from Hodgkin's disease have more general symptoms such as feeling tired, itching, rash, and loss of appetite. Night sweats, fever, and weight loss can also occur.

NON-HODGKIN'S LYMPHOMA

Non-Hodgkin's lymphoma affects around 20 out of every 100,000 people in the United States. All types of lymphoma that don't involve R-S cells are grouped into the broad category of non-Hodgkin's lymphoma. Non-Hodgkin's lymphoma can result from the malignant growth of various types of lymphocytes. Leukemia is another type of cancer that occurs when cells in the bloodstream grow out of control. Similar uncontrolled growth of lymphocytes occurs in non-Hodgkin's lymphoma and a type of leukemia called acute lymphoblastic leukemia (ALL). That is why it can sometimes be difficult to tell the difference between non-Hodgkin's lymphoma and leukemia.

One type of non-Hodgkin's lymphoma is called Burkitt's lymphoma. This type of non-Hodgkin's lymphoma is most often found in young people between the ages of twelve and thirty. It usually takes the form of a rapidly growing tumor in the abdomen. Burkitt's lymphoma is rare in the United States and Canada, but it is the most common type of cancer seen in children in central Africa. Some researchers have suggested that there is a link between certain types of non-Hodgkin's lymphoma, such as Burkitt's lymphoma, and the Epstein-Barr virus, which causes infectious mononucleosis, or mono. This connection is based on research that has found pieces of genes from the Epstein-Barr virus in some cancer cells taken from non-Hodgkin's lymphoma patients.

CLASSIFYING NON-HODGKIN'S LYMPHOMA

Over the past forty years, many attempts have been made to develop a system for classifying non-Hodgkin's lymphomas. Understanding how the different types of non-Hodgkin's lymphomas originate can help us

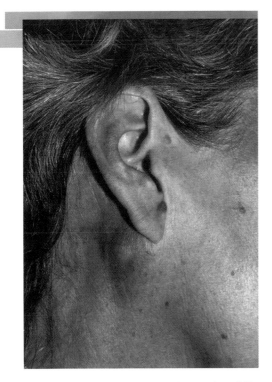

A swollen lymph node is recognizable behind and below the ear on this patient's neck. Due to being deeply imbedded in connective tissue, the most common areas where swollen lymph nodes can be felt are where they are clustered—the neck, groin, and the back of the head.

understand the best way to manage the disease. Various types of non-Hodgkin's lymphoma originate in different ways, behave in different ways, and have different chances of being cured. Any classification system for the disease must be regularly updated as new treatments are developed and new information becomes available from the field of immunology (the study of the immune system), histology (the study of the structure and functioning of cells), and genetics.

In 1993, prominent histopathologists (experts who study diseases in cells) from the United States, Europe, and Asia joined to form the International Lymphoma Study Group. This group published a joint European-American classification of lymphoid tumors called the REAL (Revised European/American Lymphoma) classification. In 2001, the World Health Organization (WHO) sponsored an update of this classification system by the Society for Haematopathology and the European Association of Haematopathology. The system classifies lymphomas according to their shape and structure as well as the type of immune cell they developed from and their genetic information. Non-Hodgkin's lymphomas fall into one of two categories: slow growing and fast growing.

SLOW-GROWING NON-HODGKIN'S LYMPHOMA

About 30 percent of non-Hodgkin's lymphomas are of types that a patient can live with for several years untreated. Because of the slow rate at which these tumors grow, these lymphomas are sometimes referred to as indolent (lazy) lymphomas. It might seem as if it would be better for a patient to have a slow-growing form of cancer rather than a fast-growing form. However, the nature of indolent lymphomas causes two problems: (1) Because they don't display obvious symptoms for so long, most patients with this type of lymphoma are not diagnosed until the disease is very far advanced, making it harder to cure, and (2) patients who go into remission (stop showing signs of the disease) as a result of treatment can experience a reoccurrence of the disease several years later. About half of those with this type of lymphoma are in a very advanced stage of the disease when they are finally diagnosed.

FAST-GROWING NON-HODGKIN'S LYMPHOMA

Some types of non-Hodgkin's lymphoma may lead to a patient's death within months. This type of non-Hodgkin's lymphoma is called aggressive non-Hodgkin's lymphoma. The most common type of aggressive non-Hodgkin's lymphoma is diffuse large cell lymphoma, which represents 30 percent of non-Hodgkin's lymphoma cases.

CUTANEOUS T CELL LYMPHOMA

A group of lymphomas that primarily affects the skin is called cutaneous T cell lymphoma. In the early phases of this disease, the only sign of this type of lymphoma may be flat, raised patches on the skin without any

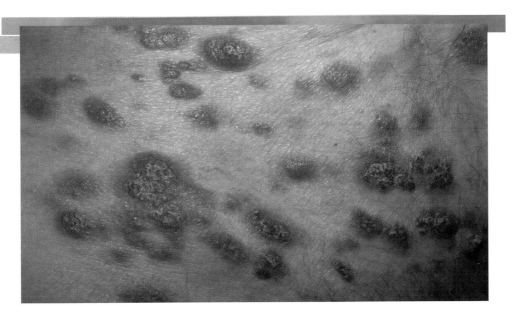

This is a close-up of cutaneous T cell lymphoma. Of all cutaneous lymphomas, 65 percent are the T cell type. A specific type of T cell gains the ability to enter the skin and circulate between the skin, the node, and blood. Then, its marker enables the T cell to tether the skin cells. This is considered a low-grade lymphoma.

tumors or organ involvement. In one type of cutaneous T cell lymphoma, Sezary syndrome, the skin appears red and abnormal cells can be found in the patient's blood. The diagnosis of skin lymphomas is sometimes difficult because this disease can look like other less serious skin diseases. Sometimes patients have skin symptoms for eight to ten years before they are diagnosed as having cutaneous lymphoma. Among patients who have been diagnosed with cutaneous lymphoma, five to ten years of survival after diagnosis is typical.

WHAT CAUSES LYMPHOMA?

Unlike some types of cancer, lymphoma is not hereditary. It results from something that disrupts the normal functions of lymphatic system cells

Studies show that 80 to 90 percent of cancers are related to environmental factors. These include ionizing radiation (for example, those survivors who developed leukemia after the dropping of the atomic bombs in Japan in 1945) and chemical carcinogens. Although the most obvious chemical carcinogen with a direct correlation to cancer is cigarette smoking, this group also includes pesticides and heavy metals (for example, lead) that are released into the environment. Here, heavy metals and other chemicals are being emptied into a river in Peru, rendering the water undrinkable as well as killing off the fish.

at some point during a person's life, rather than a defect that is passed from parent to child. Most lymphomas are the result of random mutations (changes) in genes that cause these cells to behave abnormally. These mutations may be caused by a number of factors. Sometimes they are caused by viruses. Viruses take over the reproductive mechanisms in the cells they infect in order to make more copies of themselves. In the process, the viruses may cut out or insert genetic material that causes the cells to behave abnormally. Exposure to toxic chemicals, drugs that suppress the immune system (such as those used after organ transplants), or radiation used for treatment for other types of cancer can also cause lymphomas.

CELLS MUST DIE

Another possible cause of lymphoma has been suggested by scientists. There may be a problem with the regulatory mechanism that causes unnecessary lymphocytes to die. Certain lymphomas are characterized by the swapping of parts of two chromosomes (the genetic information-carrying component of cells), causing the fusion of two previously distinct genes. One type of these chromosomal translocations leads to the over-production of a particular protein called bcl-2. This protein interferes with the normal process of cell death, which normally leads lymphocytes that are not being used to die off. Since the lymphocytes do not die, more and more of them build up in the lymphatic system.

TOO MUCH STIMULATION

Many scientists think there is a link between the level of activity in the immune system and lymphomas. Studies of lymphomas in AIDS (acquired immunodeficiency syndrome) patients are contributing to our knowledge of how lymphomas may come about. AIDS is a disorder in which people's immune system cells are disrupted by certain virus particles. The immune system then loses its ability to fight off other

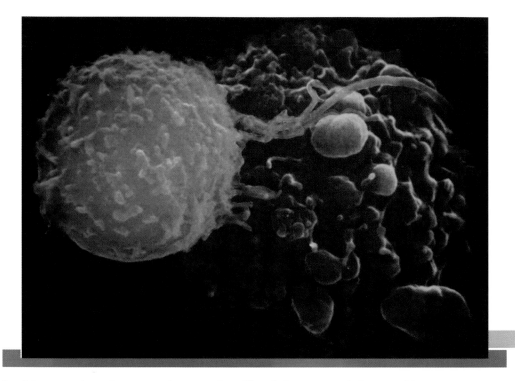

In this scanning electron micrograph, a T cell (in orange) is attacking a cancer cell, causing it to succumb to programmed cell death, or apoptosis. The mauve vessels coming from the cancer cell indicate that this process is under way. The understanding of this natural process of cell death may lead to the use of apoptosis strategically to treat cancer in the future.

infections. Lymphoma is one of the diseases frequently found in people who have AIDS. The link between AIDS and lymphoma has led some researchers to suggest that the constant stimulating of the immune system, for example by the AIDS virus, leads to so many changes within immune system cells that this eventually results in defective cells that grow out of control.

The idea that there is a link between overstimulation of the immune system and lymphoma is supported by the fact that people with other types of autoimmune diseases (diseases in which a person's immune system cells attack his or her own body) also have a greater chance of developing lymphoma. As with the AIDS virus, the immune systems of people with autoimmune diseases are constantly being stimulated—this time by the presence of one's own normal cells. This link between overstimulation of the immune system and the production of defective lymphocytes may provide an important clue in the search for ways of treating lymphoma.

CHAPTER

4

THE TREATMENT OF LYMPHOMA

When lymphoma is suspected, a doctor will do a complete physical of the patient and obtain a medical history. If the doctor finds a swollen gland and is concerned that it might be the sign of a lymphoma, he or she often will perform a biopsy. In this procedure, the doctor inserts a hollow needle into the node and removes some cells or makes a small cut and removes a little bit of the tissue. The tissue sample is sent to a laboratory, where the cells are examined to see if they are normal or abnormal. In addition, if the cells turn out to be abnormal, the laboratory examination can reveal the specific type of cancer cell that is present, and thus the type of lymphoma. Other more complex tests, such as genetic studies, are then done to determine exactly what type of lymphoma the patient has.

It is also important to establish exactly which parts of the body are affected by the disease. In order to find this out, doctors use tests such as:

— Blood tests to evaluate if the liver and kidneys are healthy, and to see if the number of red and white blood cells in the patient's bloodstream is normal.

— A biopsy of the patient's bone marrow to see if the cells being produced in the patient's bone marrow are normal in structure and number.

— A spinal tap (or lumbar puncture as it's known in medical terminology) in which a small amount of spinal fluid is removed from the patient and examined to see if the cancer cells have spread to the brain or spinal cord.

— An ultrasound, in which a device bounces sound waves off organs that have possibly been affected, to produce an image of the organ on a computer monitor that the doctor can examine for signs of abnormality.

— X-rays, computed tomography (CT) or magnetic resonance imaging (MRI) scans, and/or a positron electron tomography (PET) scan. These are all methods that use radiation or magnetic fields to produce an image of the inside of the patient's body on film that the doctor can examine.

— A bone scan to look for evidence of tumors or inflammation in the bones.

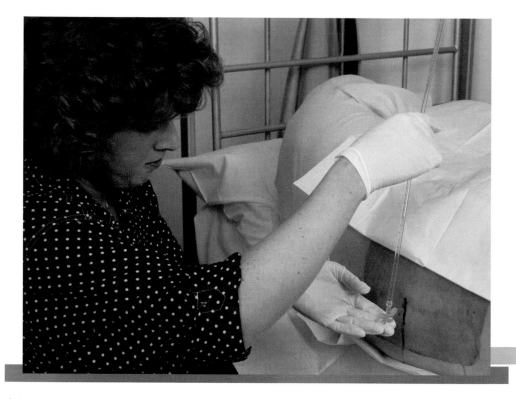

A lumbar puncture, or spinal tap, is being performed here. The cerebrospinal fluid is extracted with a hollow needle, most often between the third and fourth lumbar vertebrae below the spine. Spinal taps may be performed in order to see if lymphoma has spread to the central nervous system or bone marrow, although this procedure for staging lymphoma is rarely called for.

Tests such as these allow doctors to figure out exactly what type of lymphoma a patient has and design a treatment that will best treat that particular type of lymphoma.

STAGING LYMPHOMA

In order to determine the outlook for the patient and the most appropriate treatment, doctors must "stage" the lymphoma. Staging is the process of determining how advanced the disease is. To stage lymphoma, doctors must determine the number of lymph nodes affected by the lymphoma and where they are located in the patient's body.

The most commonly used methods of staging lymphoma are variants of the Ann Arbor staging system, which is named after the location of the conference at which it was adopted in 1974. In this system, the lymphoma is described as being in one of four stages:

Stage I In this stage, the lymphoma is only present in lymph nodes in one area of the body (such as the left armpit), or only in one non-lymph-node organ. People with this stage of lymphoma have the greatest chance for successfully recovering from the disease.

Stage II In this stage, the lymphoma is present in two or more groups of lymph nodes on the same side of the diaphragm (the large muscle under the rib cage that goes up and down when you breathe) or in one organ and lymph node group on the same side of the diaphragm.

Stage III In this stage, the lymphoma affects groups of lymph nodes on both sides of the diaphragm and sometimes the spleen or non-lymphatic-system organs as well.

Stage IV In this stage, the patient has an advanced form of the disease, and multiple organs or a single organ, the bone marrow, and distant lymph nodes are affected.

In the past, when staging showed that a patient had lymphoma in the upper part of the body, doctors would do a surgical exploration of the

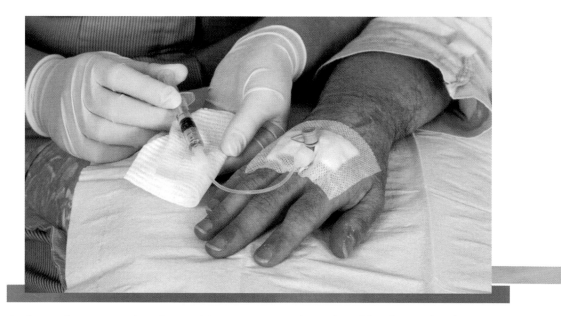

A chemotherapy patient is receiving treatment through a blood vessel in his hand. It may soon be possible for cancer patients to receive chemotherapy treatment in the comfort of their own home. New ways around drug resistance are being researched, including drug-induced apoptosis of cancer cells. This would involve blockading the survival signaling protein that leads to drug resistance.

patient's abdomen to make sure there were no microscopic tumors there. However, this exploration is not done in all cases nowadays, because the discovery of such a tumor doesn't change the type of treatment used.

After lymphoma is diagnosed, it must be treated. There are two major types of treatment used for lymphoma: radiation (exposure to X-rays) and chemotherapy (treatment with toxic drugs or chemicals). The following sections describe the history of these two types of treatment.

RADIATION TREATMENT

Before the twentieth century, patients with lymphoma were simply treated for the symptoms they experienced as a result of the disease.

This was an attempt to make them more comfortable until they died. Before Wilhelm Conrad Röntgen discovered X-rays in 1896, the only approach for treating cancer directly was surgical removal of obvious tumors. After Röntgen's discovery, many doctors became interested in the possibility of using the newly discovered X-rays to treat various diseases. In 1902, W. A. Pusey was the first to use X-rays to treat lymphomas. This was the beginning of nonsurgical approaches to treating cancer. Because the treatments resulted in a rapid and significant reduction in the size of tumors, Pusey's work provided encouragement for the further use of radiation treatment in cancer therapy in general. Throughout the first two decades of the twentieth century, scientists such as Marie Curie, codiscoverer of the radioactive element radium; William David Coolidge, who developed an improved filament (a thin wire) made of tungsten for X-ray tubes, which allowed for more consistent and better quality X-ray pictures; and other scientists contributed to improved X-ray technology. This increased its value as a tool for medical treatment and allowed it to be applied more precisely.

IMPROVING RADIATION THERAPY

A Swiss radiation therapist, Rene Gilbert, is generally credited with being the first to implement modern radiation therapy for lymphoma. Gilbert was the first to observe that lymphoma spreads in an orderly fashion from the site at which it starts to adjacent sites, then to the next nearest sites, and so on. Gilbert established two basic principles of radiation treatment: (1) kill all the cancer at one time with the first course of radiation, and (2) carefully evaluate the patient to find all the sites where there is cancer, and develop a systematic plan for irradiation, or exposure of the patient to radiation in order to kill cancer cells. He noticed that when X-ray treatment was concentrated only on areas obviously affected, the lymphoma often came back. Therefore, he advocated treating not only the areas obviously affected by lymphoma, but those nearby

Here, a man with Hodgkin's disease undergoes radiation therapy on a linear accelerator. He is to receive treatment on the areas illuminated on his chest. The lead blocks suspended overhead serve to block the radiation from the lungs. Linear accelerators produce high-energy radiation beams that deliver the radiation deep into the tissue where the cancer is located. This state-of-the-art technique is an improvement on targeting tumors and reduces side effects for the patient.

areas apparently not yet affected. In 1948, using segmental radiation (radiation used on specific areas, or segments, of the body) Gilbert and L. Babaiantz were able to demonstrate prolonged survival in a group of patients. Their success stimulated an increased interest in the application of radiation to treating cancer.

ADVANCING LYMPHOMA TREATMENT

The importance of radiation therapy became truly apparent in the 1950s. Canadian radiologist Vera Peters (1911–1993) played a key role in establishing the usefulness of radiation as a cancer treatment. Peters's research advanced lymphoma treatment in a number of ways. First, Peters and Henry Kaplan studied the clinical histories of a large number of patients with Hodgkin's disease. From the data they obtained, they were able to map the pattern that Hodgkin's disease followed as it spread. Understanding these patterns allowed them to apply radiation in appropriate patterns to treat the disease.

In addition, Peters developed a staging system that categorized a patient's lymphoma not only according to the anatomical pattern of the disease, but also according to systemic symptoms such as fever that the patient experienced. She was also a pioneer in treating lymphoma with radiation. As a result of her improved diagnostic procedures as well as her emphasis on applying radiation in appropriate patterns, 51 percent of her patients survived five years after treatment and 25 percent survived for ten years. Eighty-eight percent of her stage I patients survived at least five years, and 72 percent of her stage II patients survived for at least five years. These five- and ten-year survival rates were so impressive that they demonstrated that radiotherapy had the ability to cure Hodgkin's disease. Peters emphasized that the location of the lymphoma was not as important a factor in patients' long-term survival as the presence or absence of systemic symptoms, gender, and age.

IMPROVED TECHNOLOGY

In the 1950s and early 1960s, improvements in the technology of radiation delivery devices paved the way for the treatment of lymphoma with high-dosage radiation. In 1951, cobalt therapy was invented, using a radioactive element called cobalt-60 as the source of the radiation beam. That same year at Stanford University, Henry Kaplan and a graduate student, Karl Brown, designed the first linear accelerator in the United States. A linear accelerator, as the name implies, speeds up the electrons used to produce energy beams. These developments resulted in high-energy beams of radiation that provide for more precise and powerful cancer treatment. The Stanford group performed a number of studies aimed at identifying the correct amount of radiation to treat tumors. Henry Kaplan started using "wide-field" radiation for stage I and II Hodgkin's disease. In this approach, as many related groups of lymph nodes as possible are treated with as few doses of high-energy radiation. Kaplan's work laid the foundation for the radiation techniques used today to treat lymphoma. Kaplan's research established the optimal pattern for radiation treatment as the "mantle" pattern, so called because it resembles the shape of a medieval knight's cape, or mantle.

In 1962, Henry Kaplan and Saul Rosenberg, one of Kaplan's colleagues at Stanford, also pioneered the approach of treating Hodgkin's disease patients with a combination of high-energy radiation and chemotherapy, which resulted in improved survival rates for these patients.

CHEMOTHERAPY

As early as 1894, the use of arsenic as a treatment for cancer is mentioned in a medical textbook by Sir William Osler (1849–1919), Canadian-born physician and chief of staff at Johns Hopkins University and hospital in Baltimore, Maryland. But the modern field of chemotherapy has its origin in the two world wars.

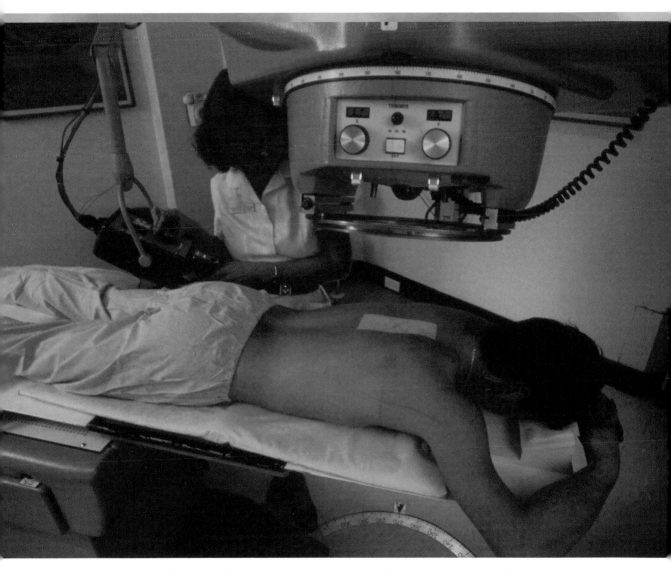

Gamma radiotherapy is less powerful than the voltage produced by linear accelerators and is often used to treat localized secondary cancers. Gamma rays are the result of the radiation released by the elements uranium, radium, and cobalt-60. In radiotherapy, cobalt-60 is the element most commonly used. Here, the cobalt is located within the head of the machine, and gamma radiation flows from a shutter when the machine is operating.

During World War I (1914–1918), mustard gas was used on the battlefield as an early form of chemical warfare. Doctors observed that soldiers who had inhaled mustard gas and suffered mustard poisoning as a result showed a dissolving of lymphatic tissue. This led some physicians to consider that it might be possible to use chemicals to destroy lymphoma.

However, the field of chemotherapy did not truly evolve until World War II (1939–1945), when an explosion in the harbor of Bari, Italy, resulted in servicemen being exposed to toxic levels of mustard gas. Observing once again that the mustard gas dissolved lymphoid tissue led two researchers at Yale University, M. J. Goodman and A. Gilman, to study its possible use in treating lymphoma. They performed a study using nitrogen mustard, a chemical derived from mustard gas. Lymphoma turned out to be very responsive to treatment with nitrogen mustard, but the results were short-lived. Still, this was a pioneering effort in single-agent chemotherapy.

THE CHEMISTRY OF LYMPHOMA THERAPY

Both arsenic and mustard gas are alkylating agents. Alkylating agents attach groups of certain molecules to cells' genetic material, or DNA (deoxyribonucleic acid). These chemicals disrupt the DNA, leading to the death of cells, which is desirable if the cells are cancer cells. In 1963, J. L. Scott published a paper on using other alkylating agents such as chlorambucil after treating patients with advanced Hodgkin's disease with nitrogen mustard. In the study, patients who received chlorambucil went three times as long before relapsing as compared to those who were only treated with nitrogen mustard. Such research sparked a search for combinations of drugs that would improve patients' survival. Throughout the 1960s, various combinations of chemical agents were tried in an effort to find a combination that would both be effective and produce lasting results.

Historically, the periwinkle plant has been used to treat a number of diseases. For example, by steeping its leaves to make tea, it can be used to improve diabetes. Yet it is most widely used now for the anticancer properties of the plant's extract. Vinca alkaloids are effective during the M (mitotic) phase of the cell cycle—causing disruption to the spindle parts. The plant grows in warm regions, particularly in the southern United States.

Progress was made in the use of alkylating agents when new agents called vinca alkaloids were discovered in plants such as the rosy periwinkle. In the 1960s, the U.S. National Cancer Institute supported a large study in which these agents were used as chemotherapy for lymphoma. A vinca alkyloid called vinblastine was used to treat Hodgkin's disease and vincristine was used to treat non-Hodgkin's lymphomas. The results of these studies established the superior effectiveness of these compounds.

Agents such as nitrogen mustard work by killing fast-growing cells such as those typical of cancer. The disadvantage of this type of chemical agent is that it kills other cells in the body besides cancer cells. Agents that kill cells are said to be cytotoxic. The first noncytotoxic substance to treat lymphoma was a corticosteroid. This is a chemical agent that causes the body to increase its production of a compound called cortisone. O. H. Pearson and the researchers working with him reported cortisone-induced improvement of Hodgkin's disease and lymphosarcoma. Many corticosteroid compounds were studied, and one called prednisone became the most widely used one for the treatment of blood-related cancers.

FINDING BETTER TREATMENTS

At the National Cancer Institute in 1963, researchers developed the first combination chemotherapy for treating advanced Hodgkin's disease by combining four anticancer agents into a regimen called MOMP. The acronym (MOMP) refers to the combination of mustard, oncovin, methotrexate, and prednisone. Eventually procarbazine was substituted for methotrexate because it was more effective, a combination that became known as MOPP. This combination resulted in 80 percent of patients going into remission, four times as many went into remission after being treated with a single chemotherapy agent. More impressively, 68 percent of treated patients were still disease free after five years, compared to only 10 percent of patients treated with a single agent.

In 1969, the first antibiotic that is found to have anticancer effects, doxorubicin, was discovered. The discovery of other antibiotics with tumor-killing properties soon followed. Since the 1970s, a variety of combinations of chemotherapy agents has been developed, resulting in impressive remission rates for many varieties of lymphoma.

In the 1980s, the use of bone marrow transplantation was pioneered as a treatment for those patients who had serious relapses of either Hodgkin's disease or non-Hodgkin's lymphoma. In this approach a patient's bone marrow, where lymphocytes are produced, is completely destroyed by exposure to strong chemotherapy agents. Once all the lymphatic cells

"MINI" BONE MARROW TRANSPLANTATION

Bone marrow transplantation has become a frequent treatment for cancers such as lymphoma. However, this form of treatment is very debilitating for the patient, because the high doses of radiation and/or chemotherapy used to kill all the cells in that person's bone marrow also affect other cells in that person's body.

Currently, a gentler approach to bone marrow transplantation for blood cancers such as lymphoma is being studied in clinical trials. This technique is callled mini-transplantation, or reduced-intensity transplantation. In this approach, lower, less-toxic doses of chemotherapy and/or radiation are used to kill some but not all of the patient's bone marrow and reduce the number of, but not eliminate, the cancer cells. Cancer-free donor bone marrow is then transplanted, and as the new marrow produces healthy cells, these cells destroy the remaining cancer cells. If this approach proves to be successful, it will make the process of bone marrow transplantation less difficult for patients.

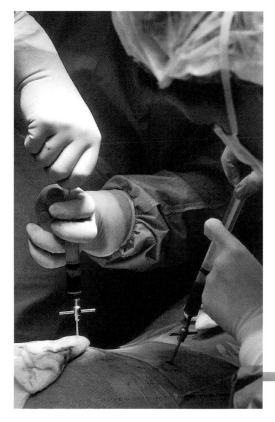

Obtaining donor bone marrow is known as harvesting. Here, a doctor performs this procedure. Marrow from a donor is usually harvested from the hip bone. The duration of this procedure is one to two hours.

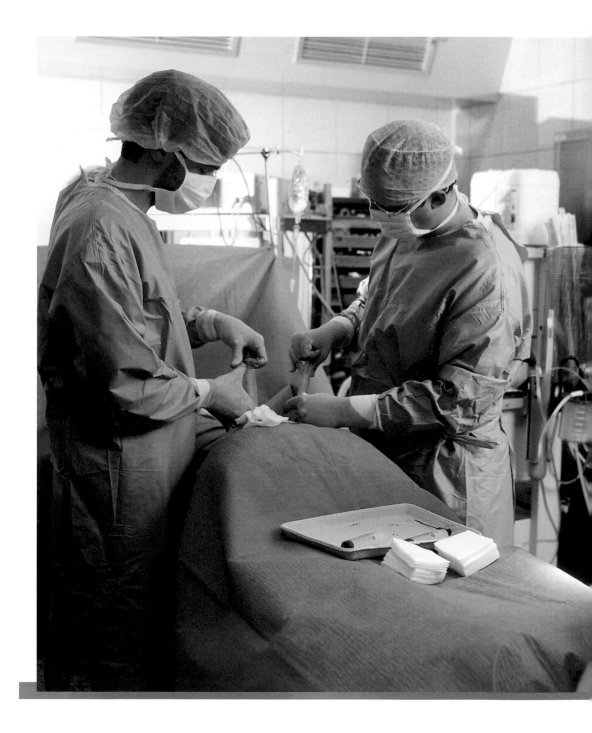

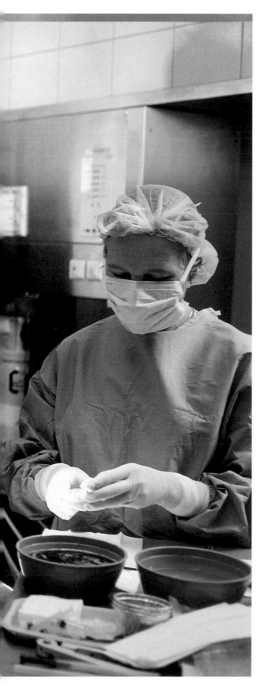

A surgical team performs a bone marrow transplant (BMT). The first successful BMT happened in 1956. In 1991, 7,500 patients nationwide underwent a BMT. Today, it is a means of saving thousands of lives and is often used aggressively rather than at later stages in treating lymphoma. If a lymphoma patient's bone marrow is cancer-free, the patient can serve as his or her own donor. This is known as an autologous BMT.

including the cancerous ones are dead, new bone marrow either saved from the patient or from a donor is reintroduced into the patient's blood stream, where it finds its way back into the bone. Once transplanted, the aim is that the marrow will start to produce new immune system and blood cells that are cancer-free. Sometimes peripheral stem cell transplantation is also used. In this technique, immature blood cells (stem cells) are taken from the blood of the patient or a donor and given to the patient after treatment. This technique helps the bone marrow to produce more healthy blood and immune system cells.

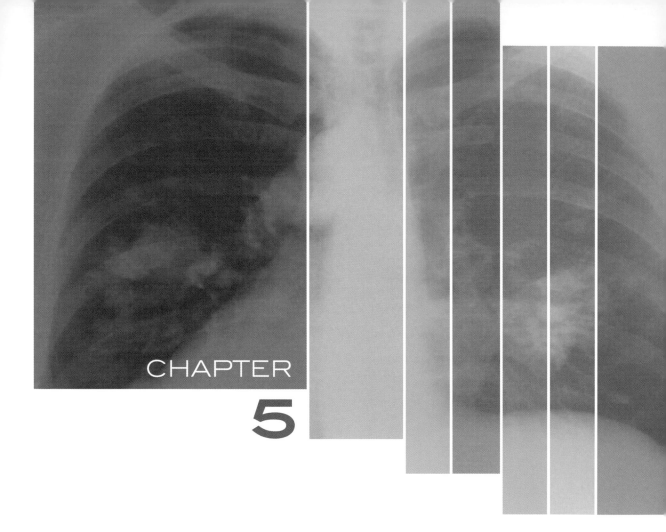

CHAPTER
5

THE FUTURE

Today not only are the five-year survival rates for lymphoma impressive, but 30 percent of lymphoma patients show no evidence of lymphoma when they eventually die from other causes. However, there is a drawback to lymphoma treatment. Although radiation is extremely successful in eliminating lymphoma, some patients who are treated with radiation eventually develop other tumors, either malignant or benign, as a result of exposure to the treatment itself. Therefore the search has continued for new and innovative treatments for lymphoma.

Researchers are continuing to search for both ways to improve existing treatments for lymphoma and to find totally new treatments that have a better chance to cure patients or produce fewer serious side effects. Since Hodgkin's disease has a high cure rate, much of the research in this area is focused on finding treatments that have fewer short-term and long-term side effects. In the area of non-Hodgkin's lymphoma, researchers are primarily concentrating on finding treatments that will result in a higher cure rate.

MONOCLONAL ANTIBODY TREATMENT

Traditionally, lymphomas have been treated with radiation therapy and/or chemotherapy. However, promising new treatments are currently being developed. One such treatment is the use of monoclonal antibodies. Monoclonal antibodies are substances that are produced by B cells and can attach themselves to cancer cells. These antibodies are "monoclonal" because they are produced in laboratories by cells that are grown from one particular cell that produces the desired antibody. One monoclonal antibody that is being used to treat indolent lymphomas is rituximab, which binds to a specific B cell antigen called CD20. After this antibody binds to the tumor cells, it makes the cells more vulnerable to chemicals used in chemotherapy. It has been successfully used to treat patients whose tumors were previously resistant to chemotherapy. In studies in the United Kingdom, rituximab treatment has demonstrated a successful remission rate of 40 to 50 percent.

CONJUGATED MONOCLONAL ANTIBODIES

Conjugated monoclonal antibodies are also being developed for treating lymphoma. These include epratuzamab, an antibody that recognizes the CD22 antigen on B cells, and alemtuzumab, which responds to the

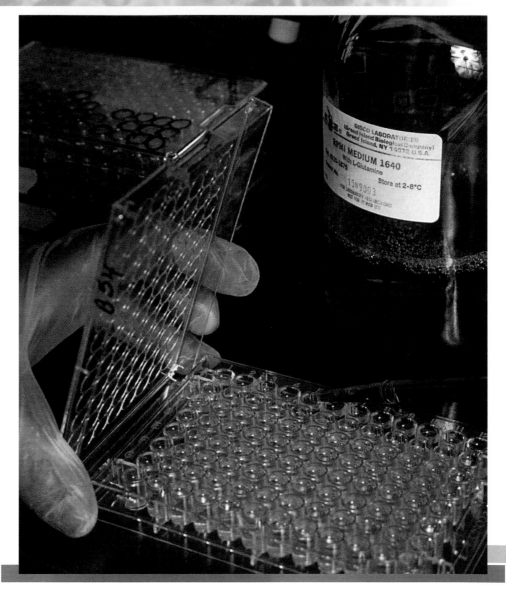

Cells that grow monoclonal antibodies are sorted and grown in wells, pictured here. They take many years and much work to develop, and will become an increasingly important treatment for lymphoma in the future. Besides the very common rituximab, effective on cancerous B cells, a radioactive antibody is being tested in clinical trials in the United Kingdom. Today, monoclonal antibodies are only effective for low-grade non-Hodgkin's, but the hope is to one day be able to treat T cell lymphomas and Hodgkin's disease.

CD52 antigen on most B and T cells. Conjugated monoclonal antibodies are those combined with another form of treatment. Such conjugated monoclonal antibodies combined with radiation or chemotherapy agents have shown promising results in tests in human beings. In these cases, the monoclonal antibodies are combined with either chemotherapy agents or radioactive elements. The antibodies are infused into the patient and travel through the patient's system until they encounter the type of cell (B cell or T cell) to which they bind. They then bind with the target cell, which is killed by the chemical or radioactive agent that is carried by the monoclonal antibody.

VACCINES

Researchers are also trying to develop vaccines that are designed to make patients resistant to tumors the same way that the polio vaccine, for instance, makes people immune to poliovirus. As genetic research has allowed specific compounds produced by cancer cells to be identified, it has become theoretically possible to activate people's own immune system to recognize, attack, and destroy the abnormal cells. Vaccines for these purposes are currently being tested in laboratories.

GENE THERAPY

Gene therapy is another area being explored to treat lymphoma. Gene therapy relies on the infusion into the patient's bloodstream of deactivated virus cells into which a gene designed for a specific purpose has been inserted. The virus particles enter the cancer cells and insert the gene they carry into the cancer cell's DNA. When the cancer cell reproduces, the new cells incorporate the implanted DNA. This new DNA either inhibits the expression of the cancer-causing gene, replaces the defective gene with a healthy gene, or initiates the production of a compound that causes the defective cell to behave in an appropriate (noncancerous) way.

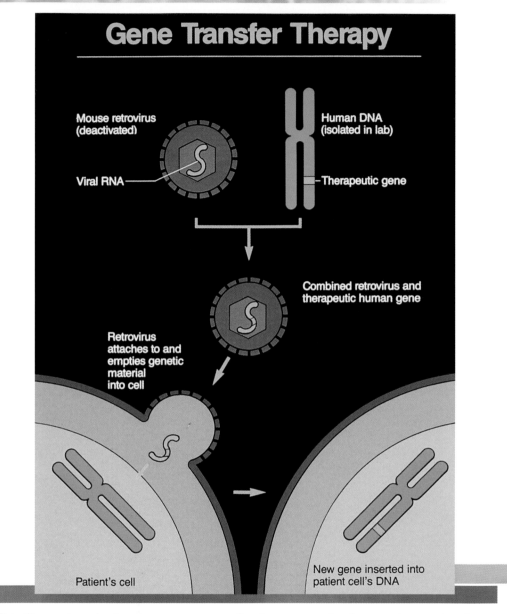

Gene Transfer Therapy

Mouse retrovirus (deactivated)

Human DNA (isolated in lab)

Viral RNA

Therapeutic gene

Combined retrovirus and therapeutic human gene

Retrovirus attaches to and empties genetic material into cell

Patient's cell

New gene inserted into patient cell's DNA

This illustration depicts how gene transfer therapy works. A retrovirus stores its genetic information on a single strand of RNA, rather than the usual double-stranded DNA, when not affecting a cell. Then, it later constructs DNA using the enzyme reverse-transcriptase. In gene therapy, a human therapeutic gene is inserted into a deactivated mouse retrovirus in the laboratory, before being integrated into the patient's DNA.

These scientists are analyzing the black bands making up the structure of human DNA sequences. By using a method to switch on a cancer cell with a marker gene, cancer cells can be specifically targeted while healthy cells are switched off. Scientists in gene therapy research are exploring how to use a genetic switch to express an anticancer gene that will then attack the cancer cells.

ANTIANGIOGENICS

Cancer cells require a large and highly complex set of blood vessels to support their out-of-control growth. Without this network of blood vessels to supply nutrients and remove waste products, cancer cannot successfully grow. This concept has spurred an interest in developing techniques that would inhibit the blood supply to tumors. However, this is a very complex process, which makes research in this area difficult.

PROTEASOME INHIBITION

Enzymes are proteins produced in the body that affect biological activities of the body. There are enzymes found in the body called proteasomes, which break down proteins found in cells. Keeping proteasomes from performing their regulatory activities in cells has been shown to result in the death of tumor cells and the inhibition of their ability to spread. Possible use of proteasome inhibitors is presently being investigated in laboratories.

HOPE FOR THE FUTURE

In the future, some or all of these new techniques will no doubt play an important role in the treatment of lymphoma. Some of these therapies will replace older therapies or be used in cases that do not respond to standard therapy. Others will be used in combination with radiation or

THE FIRST MONOCLONAL ANTIBODY TREATMENT FOR LYMPHOMA

Researchers are actively seeking new and improved approaches to treating lymphoma. In 1997, Rituxan, manufactured by Genentech Corporation, became the first monoclonal antibody to be approved for the treatment of lymphoma by the U.S. Food and Drug Administration. Rituxan, whose generic name is rituximab, is used to treat a type of B cell lymphoma. Rituxan works by attaching itself to a location on the B cell lymphocyte called the CD20 antigen. The fact that the medication is designed to attach only to this site means that it can specifically target lymphoma cells. An advantage of monoclonal antibody treatment is that side effects are usually milder with this treatment than with conventional chemotherapy. Nearly half of the patients in clinical trials with Rituxan experienced full or complete improvement in their lymphoma. The potential of this type of therapy has sparked a great deal of interest in the medical community, and it is being used in more than 200 present and planned clinical trials.

chemotherapy to improve a patient's chances of survival. Still others will be used as maintenance therapies after the patient's tumors have been killed by high-dose radiation or chemotherapy to ensure that the patient remains cancer free. There is little doubt that treatments and survival rates will continue to advance throughout the next few decades, offering the hope of better chances of survival, longer life, and improved quality of life for those suffering from lymphoma.

GLOSSARY

autoimmune disease A type of disorder in which the immune system mistakenly attacks a person's healthy cells.

benign tumor An abnormal clump of cells that does not invade tissue or spread to other parts of the body.

cadaver A dead body, especially one intended for study or transplantation.

cytotoxic Relating to a substance that has a toxic effect to cells.

diaphragm The large muscle that separates the area above the rib cage from the abdomen.

gene A segment of DNA that carries the blueprint for a specific compound in the body.

hormone A chemical that regulates a biological function.

lymphatic system A network of organs and vessels that produces and circulates cells that protect us from foreign microorganisms.

lymphocyte A cell in the lymphatic system.

malignant tumor An abnormal clump of cells that grows out of control and spreads to other parts of the body.

morphology The structure and shape of something, such as a cell.

mutation A change in the structure of a gene.

pathology The direct study of the nature, causes, and effects of disease.

proto-oncogene A gene that becomes a cancer-causing gene if it is damaged.

receptor A component on a cell that allows it to attach, or bind with, another cell or chemical molecule.

remission A state in which a patient stops showing signs of a disease. Patients must be in remission for a certain period of time before they are considered to be cured.

segmental radiation Radiation used on specific areas, or segments, of the body.

staging The classification of how advanced a disease is.

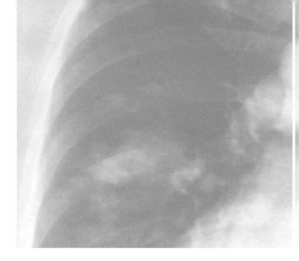

FOR MORE INFORMATION

American Cancer Society
15999 Clifton Road, NE
Atlanta, GA 30329-4251
(800) 227-2345
Web site: http://www.cancer.org

WEB SITES

Due to the changing nature of Internet links, The Rosen Publishing Group, Inc., has developed an online list of Web sites related to the subject of this book. This site is updated regularly. Please use this link to access the list:

http://www.rosenlinks.com/cms/lymp

FOR FURTHER READING

Gifford, Rebecca. *Cancer Happens: Coming of Age with Cancer*.
    Sterling, VA: Capital Books, 2003.

Holman, Peter, Jodi Garrett, and William D. Jansen. *100 Questions
    and Answers about Lymphoma*. Boston, MA: Jones & Bartlett
    Publishers, 2003.

Starr, Janie. *The Bone Marrow Boogie: The Dance of a Lifetime*.
    Vashon Island, WA: Kota Press, 2002.

Weinberg, Robert A. *One Renegade Cell: How Cancer Begins*. New
    York, NY: Basic Books, 1998.

What You Need to Know about Hodgkin's Disease. Washington, DC:
    National Cancer Institute, 1999.

What You Need to Know about Non-Hodgkin's Lymphoma.
    Washington, DC: National Cancer Institute, 1999.

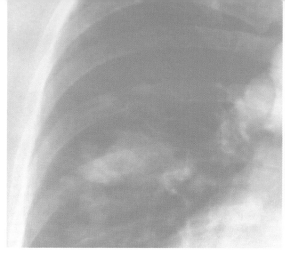

BIBLIOGRAPHY

Amini, Rose-Marie. "Hodgkin Lymphoma: Studies of Advanced Stages, Relapses and the Relation to Non-Hodgkin Lymphomas." Faculty of Medicine, University of Uppsala, Sweden, 2002.

Emory University. "Lymphomas." Retrieved September 24, 2004 (http://www.emoryradiationoncology.org/diseases-and-procedures/weblymphomas.htm).

Evans, Linda S., and Barry W. Hancock. "Non-Hodgkin Lymphoma." *The Lancet*, 362:9378, July 12, 2002, pp. 139–146.

Genentech. "History of Lymphoma." Retrieved September 23, 2004 (http://www.historyoflymphoma.com/home.html).

"GP Clinical: Behind the Headlines—New Cancer Risk After Hodgkin's." *GP*, November 24, 2003, pp. 49–51.

Lymphoma Information Network. "Hodgkin's Disease—Historical Timeline." Retrieved April 12, 2004 (http://www.lymphomainfo.net/hodgkins/timeline.html).

"Mildred Vera Peters: A Pioneering Canadian Radiotherapist," in
      Proceedings of the 10th Annual History of Medicine Days (W.A.
      Whitelaw, ed.), University of Toronto, Canada, 2001.
Radstone, Sammy. "Beyond the Name," *StudentBMJ*, Vol. 11, August 2003.
University of Maryland Medicine. "Non-Hodgkin's Lymphoma."
      Retrieved on April 12, 2004 (http://www.umm.edu/blood/
      nonhodg.htm).
Weinberg, Robert A. *One Renegade Cell: How Cancer Begins*. New York,
      NY: Basic Books, 1998.
Whonamedit.com. "Thomas Hodgkin." Retrieved on September 23,
      2004 (http://www.whonamedit.com/doctor.cfm/1495.html).
Wikipedia. "The Lymphatic System." Retrieved on April 12, 2004
      (http://en.wikipedia.org/wiki/Category:Lymphatic_system).
Wilkins, Bridget S. "Historical Review of Hodgkin's Disease." *British
      Journal of Haematology*, Vol. 117, pp. 265–274, 2002.
Yung, Lynny, and David Linch. "Hodgkin's Lymphoma (Seminar)." *The
      Lancet*, 361:9361, March 15, 2003, pp. 943–964.

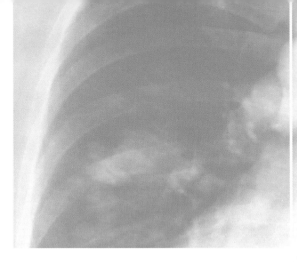

INDEX

ABOUT THE AUTHOR

Jeri Freedman has a BA from Harvard University and spent fifteen years working in companies in the biomedical and high-technology fields. She is the author of a number of other nonfiction books published by Rosen Publishing as well as several plays and, under the name Foxxe, is the coauthor of two science-fiction novels. She lives in Boston.

PHOTO CREDITS

Cover © Dr. Andrejs Liepins/Science Photo Library; cover corner photo © PunchStock; back cover and throughout © National Cancer Institute; p. 5 © David McNew/Getty Images; p. 8 © J. Bavosi/Photo Researchers; p. 10 © Science Photo Library; pp. 11, 27, 43 © Custom Medical Stock Photo, Inc.; p. 13 © NYC Franklin Research Fund/Phototake; p. 16 © John Karapelou, CMI/Phototake; p. 17 © Francis Leroy, Biocosmos/Photo Researchers, Inc.; p. 18 © Nibsc/Photo Researchers, Inc.; p. 25 © Dr. P. Marazzi/Photo Researchers, Inc.; p. 28 © Racimos de Ungurahui/AP/Wide World Photos; p. 30 © Dr. Andrejs Liepins/Photo Researchers, Inc.; pp. 34, 36, 45 © BSIP Boucharlat/Science Photo Library; pp. 38, 41 © Martin Dohrn/Photo Researchers, Inc.; pp. 46–47 © Beranger/Photo Researchers, Inc.; p. 50 © Linda Bartlett/National Cancer Institute; p. 52 © Jeannie Kelly/National Cancer Institute; p. 53 © James King-Holmes/ICRF/Photo Researchers, Inc.

Designer: Evelyn Horovicz; Editor: Leigh Ann Cobb
Photo Researcher: Hillary Arnold